THREE SCROOGES

A HOLIDAY REVERSE HAREM EROTIC SHORT

R. B. FIELDS

Copyright 2021

This book is a work of fiction. Names, characters, businesses, places, events and incidents are either the products of the author's imagination or used fictitiously. Any resemblance to actual persons, living or dead, or actual events is purely coincidental. Opinions expressed are those of the characters and do not necessarily reflect those of the author.

No part of this book may be reproduced, stored in a retrieval system, scanned, or transmitted or distributed in any form or by any means electronic, mechanical, photocopied, recorded or otherwise without written consent of the author. All rights reserved.

Distributed by Pygmalion Publishing, LLC

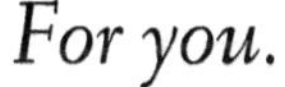

For you.

THREE STOOGES

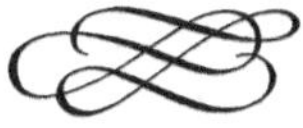

I take the last sip of eggnog that's more brandy than nog and set the cup on the nightstand, listening to the screaming wind. Ice spits against the windows, a vicious hissing brutality—Christmas Eve already, though it hardly feels like it. I have no family worth mentioning, and I kicked my boyfriend out last week—I don't even have a dog to shower with gifts. I'm not lonely, though. I love being alone. There is a simplicity to the holidays this year that's incredibly peaceful. I didn't have to put up a tree, no cleaning up pine needles, no tinsel stuck to my shoes. Glitter is the herpes of the holidays. Prove me wrong.

I did put out the electric candles my mother gave me years ago, making the living room glow yellow—warm and cozy. I also hung a spring of mistletoe in the living room doorway. A poisonous addition to the house, kinda like my ex. The biggest gift I gave myself—the only gift I gave myself outside of that egg nog—was to kick him out.

I punch the pillow to fluff it up and lay back with enough force to make the bed squeak. I take a deep breath and drag my fingers down over my breasts and between my legs, leaving feathery trails of sensation prickling on my flesh. I'm already wet. I haven't had sex in months, well before I told Clark to take a hike. I screw my eyes closed and imagine I'm in a doctor's office where all the men are focused on pleasing me...wait, no, a lawyer's office. Men powerful enough to take anything they want, and all they want is my wanton flesh.

Yeah, it's weird sleeping alone, but the

upside is that I can tickle the turnip whenever I want. Merry Christmas to me.

The bed squeaks again. Wait, no...that's not the bed.

I push myself to seated. *What is that noise?*

The squeak isn't coming from the bedroom at all—downstairs. The...drawers in the kitchen?

Dammit. It's Clark, back to get his corkscrew, or maybe he thinks he's entitled to the dishes—he isn't. I can hear him now, his stupid excuses: *What am I supposed to fuckin' eat off, Lexi? You have enough cash to spare a few plates.*

I sigh, kick the blankets off my legs, and shove my feet into a pair of slippers. I'm halfway across the room when the chill against my bare flesh reminds me that I need a robe, too, unless I want to give him an eye full of tit—and he has not earned the right to see me naked. Not ever again.

I ease the door open and quietly make my way up the hall to the stairway; I'd rather not alert him to my presence before I can see what he's looking for. I skip the third step down—it creaks—and round the corner at the bottom landing. The living room glows merrily, the electric candles gilding the soft leather of the couch and making the wooden end table shine.

Clark stands with his back to me, just beyond the jaundiced haze of candlelight, a black hat covering his head and ears, barely visible in the silvered haze of moonlight that leaks through the living room's bay windows. He's hunched over the odds-and-ends drawer in the foyer table. I frown. What is he looking for? The only thing in there is...

Oh shit. Is he trying to steal my car? Not today, fuck-o.

I tiptoe into the middle of the room and plant myself in front of the couch. "Get the fuck out of here, Clark, before I call the cops."

He jolts to standing quickly, the drawer slamming shut at his hip. I realize my mistake immediately. My lungs stop working, and my heart ratchets into a frenzied dance of fear. Not Clark. Clark is barely taller than

I am, spindly and thick through the belly, but this man has a foot on us both. And as he turns and steps into the living room toward me, I can see the sharp planes of his high cheekbones, the rugged five-o'clock shadow along his jaw, the deep umber of his dark eyes. I can also see the gun he has in his hand.

He steps toward me, the barrel aimed at my chest.

Uh oh.

I raise my hands in surrender—*of course; of fucking course*—but the man with the gun does not seem to want to hurt me. His eyes are wide, his mouth tight but not angry. He's surprised, yes, maybe willing to kill someone if they came at him with a weapon, but he'd rather everyone get out of here alive. Even the hammering of my heart isn't really fearful—at least, it's not all fear. He's gorgeous. A movie star playing a gunman.

"Take what you want," I snap, but it comes out harsher than I intended. I'm suddenly too annoyed to be frightened. The night was already bullshit, the scraps of pleasure I was trying to scrape together in the bedroom gone—interrupted. What does he want, my fucking toaster? *Go ahead, jerk, add insult to injury, take away my ability to make a lame-ass solo Christmas breakfast.*

"Where are all your presents?" he says, but it comes out too quiet and kind to feel threatening. And he's not watching me any-more—he averted his eyes like he's ashamed. He glances at the gun, startles as if he's just realized it's in his hand, and lowers the weapon.

"I don't have any presents. You've stum-bled into the most pathetic house on the en-tire block. Way to remind me, Scrooge."

He frowns, eyes still cast downward. Aren't robbers supposed to at least watch their hostages? Wait...am I a hostage? It sure doesn't feel like it.

I should be scared, I should say, "I have a boyfriend, he'll be home any minute!" But the fact that he broke into my house and can't even look at me is pissing me off. It's the same shit Clark used to pull when he was lying. Avoiding my eyes as if the twitch in his left eyelid was his only tell.

"At least have the decency to look at my face while you rob me," I snap.

He puts the weapon in the back of his pants and finally draws his gaze to my mine, then gestures to my chest. "You have a... wardrobe issue."

I glance down. The robe must have come untied when I raised my hands. My breasts are pale in the candlelight, nipples practically glowing. And now I can feel the wetness between my legs, remnants from my session upstairs, slipping over the tops of my inner thighs.

I should close the robe. I should play modest. But the pink flush of his cheeks, the heat on his neck... He took away my fantasy, that asshole. Maybe he can give me the real thing.

My eyes flick to the mistletoe, hanging just out of reach in the archway. It's a risk, but Christmas is a time for leaps of faith. "I could call the police," I say.

He swallows hard, the blush in his

cheeks intensifying—yeah, he's not cut out for this outlaw game. He needs someone else to tell him what to do.

"Do you want to call the police?" he asks.

"I haven't decided. Perhaps I'd be inclined to let it go if you pay for what you did." I slip the robe off my shoulders and let it drop to the floor. Then I close the distance between myself and the archway, reach up, and tug the mistletoe free.

The man watches me as I return to the living room, his eyes hooded with desire—caressing me with his gaze. I raise the plant and wiggle it.

He cocks his head, confused. "You want a...kiss?"

I smile and lower the mistletoe to a spot just above my right breast. His eyes widen—hesitation. But then I nod. "Now. Before I change my mind."

He approaches slowly, tugging the knit hat off his head to reveal short-cropped brown hair. He stops in front of me, puts his hands behind his back, and locks his fingers together as if he's putting himself in hand-cuffs. Oh yes, I could get used to this.

The heat of him—his nearness—makes my pulse race, the blood throbbing through my chest and lower, harder between my legs. He looks down at me. He glances at the plant. "Your wish is my command." Then he drops to his knees in front of me and lowers his face to my chest.

I gasp when his mouth finds my nipple, the sensual massage of his tongue raising gooseflesh on my arms. But a banging near the back of the house makes me turn—the garage door. Shoes squeal on the kitchen tile. "Look at this thing!"

Someone else is here. Did he find something to steal? But when he passes through the arch and into the living room, I can't see anything of value. The second man is as tall as his partner and even more muscular, his hair a deep red like flames, eyes a vibrant green. The only thing he's carrying is a giant icicle, one of the ones hanging from the garage door. But because of the way the plants grow up along that side of the house, the icicle is rounded on either side —smooth.

And then he sees me. He freezes, the icicle held aloft like a small branch. "Dominic, what's...uh..."

Dominic backs up just enough to speak, but his lips tickle my skin as he says: "The lady of the house had a request, Blaze. I honestly forgot you guys were here."

"You...guys?" I whisper. How many are there? And then I see number three step into the archway behind the redhead. Tattoos on his neck. Dark hair in a ponytail. Blue eyes like the ocean set deep in his face. Taller than all of them, and he has one strange addition—instead of a black knit cap, he's wearing a Santa hat.

Dominic lowers his lips to my breast once again as if I hadn't spoken. The redhead in the doorway—Blaze—looks from Dominic to me to the icicle and back again as if unsure what to do. But I know. I glance at the couch, then back to the pair in the doorway.

I raise my hand and aim a finger at Blaze,

then the man behind him. "Clothes off." I nod to the icicle—thick and opaque. "And bring that."

Blaze looks at the tattooed man, who smiles with straight white teeth. He already has his jacket off and is pulling at his T-shirt as if he's suddenly realized it's a cloth prison that he has to escape from.

Dominic chuckles.

I slap the top of his head. "Did I tell you that you could laugh?" *What am I doing?* But it feels right.

The chuckle dies in his throat. "No ma'am," he says.

I step away from him, and he leans forward after me, trying to capture my nipple once more, but I have something else in mind. I lower myself onto the couch and stretch out on my side, my top leg cocked upward. I lower my fingers to my sex, spreading myself wide, then slide a finger into my pussy.

The men watch with unbridled fascination, tearing the rest of their clothes from their flesh. All some version of well-muscled, with rippling abs, biceps that could carry you to bed with ease, and a V-shape with treasure trails leading to the dark thatches of hair around their groins. They're the kind of men who probably spend a lot of time in a prison weight room—fine, maybe a gym, but I'm going with the outlaw fantasy, though only one is covered in tattoos. He's inked from his neck all the way down to his thick cock, the thing already standing at attention. All of them are hard—all of them.

I point to Dominic, then lower the mistletoe over my breasts again. He drops to his knees in front of the couch and goes back to his task, teasing the nub of my nipple into a stiff peak.

Then I point to Blaze, smiling to myself when his dick twitches in response to my attention, and lower the mistletoe between my legs. Blaze drops to his knees beside his partner, licks his lips, then glances at the icicle, still held in his palm, melting, dripping from his fist. He watches my face as he raises the ice to my rib cage near Dominic's flicking tongue.

The cold wetness against my fevered torso is a welcome reprieve, a chill that calms the frantic pulsing of my heart just enough to allow me to take a deep breath. He slips the ice lower, over my navel, letting the water pool in my belly button for just a moment before slipping the icicle over the mound of hair between my legs. The tattooed Santa looks on from his spot behind the others. Watching—waiting for me to tell him what to do—and that alone is so fucking sexy that I feel like my skin might literally be on fire. My pussy is throbbing with need. And I'm going to make them take care of it— take care of me. It's the least they can do.

Blaze spreads my lower lips with his thumb and index finger, then slowly, achingly slowly, moves the ice into position.

The cold is brutal and intense, but as he moves it back and forth over my clit, the sensation shivers into my nerve endings—almost painful but not quite, just a throbbing intensity that accelerates with his movements until I'm pulsing my hips up to meet each stroke. Dominic, apparently deciding that fingers are allowed and maybe even pre-ferred, raises one hand from behind his back to tease my other nipple.

Blaze lowers his hand to capture my chilled clitoris between his thumb and fore-finger, then slides the icicle lower, slipping it into my pussy. I gasp at the shock of it, my insides shivering not only with pleasure but with the raw intensity of the ice. But with Blaze's fingers working my clit, and Dominic working my nipples, the cold inside me keeps the other sensations from being over-powering. That wintery bite gives me a con-crete place to focus.

Blaze works the ice in deeper, then switches the pinching, rolling motion to a gentle flicking against my clit. Then he lowers his tongue to lap at my pussy.

I moan, the throbbing beat of my heart sending frosty sleet through my nerves as if the cold from the icicle is spreading directly into my bloodstream. But the chill is easing, melting, smaller with every second that he fucks me. I feel the wetness from the water slipping from my depths and into the crack of my ass.

But I need more. I need... I raise my eyes to the man in the back of the room, still standing, the way Dominic was, with his hands behind his back, his cock on full display. Just waiting for instructions.

And boy, do I have instructions for him.

I'm gripping the mistletoe so hard between my thumb and forefinger that it's leaving deep grooves in my fingertips. I toss the plant, and the tattooed man follows it with his eyes. I point at him. "Condoms in the kitchen, Santa. Then I want you on this couch. Behind me."

He grins. Then he's gone.

Blaze's tongue is working overtime between my legs; he twists the icicle. It's smaller now from the heat of my body, a gentle, slippery chill tugging at the front wall of my vagina.

The rustling of the condom wrapper almost pushes me over the edge, but I reach down and grab Blaze's red hair in one fist and pull his mouth away from me, though he keeps the icicle moving, fucking me with frost. "Wait," I gasp. "Just...give me a second." Dominic raises his mouth from my chest, licking his lips. Blaze stops moving the ice, though he leaves it inside me. The sudden cessation of movement is intolerable. A throbbing ache tightens my insides almost immediately, pulsing and angry and awful.

And then I feel the pressure on the back of the couch, my body jostling as the tattooed man climbs onto the leather cushions behind me, my ass nestled into his groin.

His chest is hot against my shoulder blades; his fingers are forged in molten steel. He grabs my leg behind the knee and tugs until I'm resting my foot on the back of the couch. I'm wide open, the ice still inside me, his latexed cock resting on my pussy lips. He reaches between my legs to finger my clit.

I quiver, every nerve ending shimmering with a bright and urgent need. The only thing keeping me in check is the cold inside me, but then Blaze slips the icicle from my depths.

They all wait. Watching.

"Fuck me," I whisper.

That's all the prodding he needs. I feel the head of his dick probing, probing, and then he slams his beautiful cock into me to the hilt.

I cry out and throw my head back against his shoulder, his heat after the ice making the sensation all the more vibrant and intense. I'm going to come in no time. But he pauses with his cock deep inside me. Waiting again for instructions?

"Don't you fucking stop," I say. "I need you to fuck me—hard. I need you all to fuck me."

He pauses one more second, and then I realize why—Blaze has lowered his lips to my clit again, Dominic at my breasts, all of them working me. With them in position, the man behind me growls, grips my thigh tighter, and then he rotates his hips, pounding his dick deep into my pussy as the tight muscles in my abdomen begin to pulse, cresting higher, faster, seeking release.

I can't take anymore. I clasp Dominic's head against my breast and scream as the orgasm rips through me. The man behind me moans too, but he's not coming—he slows his pace to match the pulsing of my hips, dragging the pleasure out into a series of trembling waves.

I'm still shuddering when he slips from inside me and rolls onto his back, taking me with him. I'm prone, using him like a bed, my legs splayed wide, his dick slick and wet between the crack of my ass. He cements me to him with his hands on either breast and rolls my nipples between his fingers.

Blaze climbs onto the couch between my legs—between our legs. He's managed to find a condom, too—they all have. And from this vantage point, I can see that Blaze's penis is angled upward. He'll hit different places than the tattooed man. He steadies himself, his hands on my inner thighs, pressing my legs apart. But like the tattooed man, he waits.

"Fuck my pussy," I demand. "Now."

Blaze thrusts his hips forward, burying himself in my cunt. The angle of his dick presses against the front wall of my vagina, catching my G-spot every time he pulls out.

The man beneath me pulses his hips too, sliding his dick along my ass, probing at my anus. He's not trying to enter me there, I don't think, but the sensation is enough to send electricity prickling up my spine.

I won't last long like this, especially not if they touch my clit.

As if he heard my thoughts, Dominic snakes his hand between my legs and uses two of his fingers to rub frantically at that spot, already so tender from my recent orgasm. Blaze pumps his hips more slowly than the tattooed man did, but it's what I need. My insides shudder, what I think is an aftershock, but then that sensation explodes through me, locking my legs, arching my back up off the man beneath me. Blaze continues to thrust slowly, slowly until the waves settle, then he slips out.

"You're so fucking wet," Blaze says.

I nod. I can't speak, not anymore. I'm panting, my insides quivering with release, but it's more than attraction or arousal—it's power. I've never come like this before, never had so many, so fast. Knowing that I'm in charge...it's deliciously erotic. I can do anything. Anything I want.

I'm still panting when I turn my head. Dominic sits beside the couch, his hand still resting at the apex of my thighs. I meet his gaze.

He pulls his fingers to my face, smears my wetness along my lips, then meets my mouth with his own.

His tongue is cold—from the ice?—but his lips are warm as he gently probes the recesses of my mouth. He tastes of mint. My breath returns. And though my muscles are still shuddering, though I feel as if I've been forged in jelly, I break the kiss, push myself off the tattooed man, and stand before Dominic.

He sticks out his tongue and kisses me down below the same way he kissed my mouth, a gentle probing action that sends chills down into my toes. But that's not what I need from him.

"Lie down," I say.

He looks up at me, his eyes wide and questioning, but he does not argue. He lays on his back on the rug. I climb on top of him, sitting on top of his cock, but I don't slide it inside. I thrust my hips, massaging him with my outer lips, wetting him with my juices. He closes his eyes for a beat longer than a blink and moans.

"I worry I won't last long after..." He gestures to the couch.

"Because watching me is too much for you?" I thrust against him again, hard enough that he gasps.

"Yes, ma'am."

"You'll last as long as I want you to," I snap. Then I reach between my legs and guide him inside me.

I start slowly, long deep thrusts that pull him all the way out before I draw him back inside. I'm still shaking, sensitive, every movement hitting those tender places in a way that makes my insides clench and my breath hitch. I feel every pulse of my hips in my nipples. I feel every inch of his cock deep inside my abdomen, trying to tease another orgasm from me.

But the most erotic part is watching the way his eyes roll back in his head. Watching the way he gasps and clenches his teeth, trying not to come. Trying not to disappoint me.

"You like to watch, don't you?" I say.

He groans, almost a whine. "Yes, ma'am," he says.

"Maybe next time, I'll tie you up," I whisper.

"Yes, ma'am."

"Damn, Dominic really likes to be told what to do," Blaze says. He and the tattooed man, still in his Santa hat, have made their way to the spot above Dominic's head, watching from a standing position, their dicks still hard and shiny inside their latex wrappers.

I grab Blaze's dick and tug—hard—and he hisses a breath. Pain. "Shut the fuck up," I snap. "One more word, and you aren't getting off at all tonight."

Blaze's eyes widen. He closes his mouth.

I release him and lower myself onto Dominic's chest, my breasts pressing against his pecs. I grind against him ever so slowly, my clit rubbing his groin. Our lips meet gently but feverishly, the heady notes of arousal thick in my nose. But he doesn't press. He doesn't probe my lips with his tongue, doesn't even grab my ass. Because I didn't tell him to.

This is my kind of man. I suppose I should reward him for it.

I press myself to sitting on his lap, the angle forcing his cock as deep as it can possibly go. I meet his eyes. Then I raise myself up and slam myself back down, fucking him, thrusting my hips, working his dick in and out, in and out, until he's whimpering, panting, the rug clenched in his desperate fists.

"Come," I whisper, fucking him harder. "Now."

He does, groaning, his eyes locked on mine, and I go over with him, the electricity shimmering into my toes and locking my back. I pulse a few more times, drawing every last tendril of ecstasy from him, and then sit back in his lap, his dick still hidden in my cunt.

Blaze smiles down at us. "Is it my turn?"

I shrug. "Maybe tomorrow. If you're lucky."

His jaw drops. "Is this...punishment?"

I smile. *Yes, it is.* I let my eyes drift from Dominic to Blaze to the tattooed Santa. All of them beautiful in their nude glory. All of them ready to listen. The way Clark never did.

I might not have use for a boyfriend. But this might be the best Christmas ever. And I'm not giving this gift up without a fight.

Did you like the sexy robbers in "Three Scrooges"? Are you a fan of Lexi's dominatrix style, the alpha vibe, the fact that they're all obsessed with one woman? You'll love the Claimed by Outlaws series! Steamy reverse harem romance with a delicious motorcycle club twist. And if you prefer vampires in

your harem, try *Beckoned*, the first novel in the Born of Darkness series. (Read on for a sneak peek!)

If you like exclusive bonus content not available anywhere else, join my reader group at rbfields.com.

TAKEN
Claimed by Outlaws, Book #1

"Reverse harem romance with a delicious motorcycle club twist."

CHAPTER 1
Isabelle

I have enough demons hiding in my soul to sink a cruise ship, but I never expected to end up here.

The dark is absolute, a heavy, wet void. I scan the basement, trying to ensure I didn't miss some crucial bit of information; a clue that might lead authorities right to me. I know why it happened—I might have earned the barred door, truth be told—but what kind of idiot thinks they can lock me up?

Jeff McCarthy, that's who. And just look at him now.

Jeff's silvery hair sparkles in the moonlight that streams through the basement window. I was supposed to meet my ex at the amusement park to pick up the last box of my stuff. Instead, I meet Colonel Moneybags, the owner of a giant tech start-up, who acted shocked as hell that I looked at him twice, despite who he was. I saw it as an opportunity when I fucked his brains out on the Ferris wheel, still tasting metal from hours of roller coasters. My preppy-boy experiment. It had backfired spectacularly.

Especially for him.

His breath catches with a growly hitch, and I freeze, my heart in my throat, but then it starts up again. Slow—achingly slow.

Just stop, I think at him. *Just stop breathing.*

The hissing gurgling continues. But the poison his bodyguard gave me should kill him soon. It should look like natural causes. Luckily, Ronnie has a soft spot for women locked in dungeons... or maybe he just hates rich guys. Either makes sense, and I don't really care which is true. I only care that he wanted to help me.

I blink at the room once more. The metal support pole in the center glints. The bed in the corner is neatly made. The mini fridge has been wiped. I rub my aching wrist; it'll bruise, but there are no scratches from where he grabbed me on his way to the cement floor. And I already took the keys, the metal sticky against my palm.

Good—I'm good. While there might be some trace of me down here, it appears clean. He didn't rape me, so I don't have to worry about my fluids being smeared all over him. I haven't had sex since the night he brought me here two months back, back when I thought *I* was playing *him.*

Whoops. My father would be disappointed by that mistake—the man taught me everything I know about the long con. But he's dead now. Just like Jeff will be within the hour.

I shove my sandy curls off my face, trying to ignore the frantic thunking of my heart against my ribs. No, there's nothing. No fluids, no sign of struggle. A single needle mark on him, sure, but I stabbed it into his hairline when he turned away from me—it won't be immediately visible unless the coroner shaves his head.

But if Ronnie screwed up, if I didn't give Jeff enough to kill him...

Go now, Isabelle; go. I have trust issues—being raised by a con man will do that—but I don't have a choice here. I have to be as far away from this house as possible when day breaks.

I back away from him and onto the dark

landing at the bottom of the basement steps, blood whooshing in my ears—I can no longer hear him breathing over the thud of my own heart. I'm out of his sphere; finally, finally, I can't see him, can't feel him inside my chest, his energy dark and dangerous and suffocating.

The door to the upper floor looms, the hazy darkness broken only by the line of yellowed light that shines beneath it. The carved wooden railing—too fancy for a basement—looks slick in the moonlight. I climb onto the steps. For one terrifying moment, I imagine him at my back, grabbing at my hair, tearing me off my feet to crack my skull on the cement. I duck instinctively. No hands grab me.

Enough.

I race up the stairs, my shoes clutched tightly in one hand, the metal keys sharp in the other, biting into my palm. The first lock clicks open with the thready hiss of oiled metal, then the second. I feel my heart shudder and stop when the third key goes sticky in the lock—*Is it the wrong one? Am I trapped with a dying man?*—but then it turns, a loud clack that jolts my heart into hyperdrive.

Free. I'm free.

But not all the way. I'm still in his home. I'm still in trouble if anyone shows up now. My father trained me to be careful, to talk in code, to cover my ass, but this? I won't beat a murder rap.

The cold marble of the foyer chills my toes, but the front door opens without a lick of trouble. The air on the porch is sweet and damp. I shove my feet into my sneakers, thankful, at least, that he kept them after our fateful first date. That he left them in the corner of the basement, teasing me for the last two months. I swear that was part of the torture, filling my days with glimpses into a world I could no longer experience. Talking to me about his life outside in explicit detail—a tease. I think he liked that I was mouthy, that I was a challenge—I saw the fire in his eyes when he thought he broke me. I've been building to that mindset for the last month just so he'd let his guard down long enough for me to escape.

The soles of my shoes make a wet noise against the sprinkler-soaked grass, but the leaves crackling at the edge of the emerald lawn are louder, skittering underfoot. The moment I step inside the tree line, the darkness cascades over me like a blanket, soothing my rattled nerves—so dark back here, but I know where I am. I know every inch of this town by heart.

But the world feels different after months of captivity—bigger, almost too expansive. The woods have never felt so alive. Creatures rustle the underbrush, squirrels, maybe, but squirrels don't come out at night. Raccoons? Bigger than squirrels for sure, and the way they're skittering around, it sounds like they're following me.

For fuck's sake, grow some ovaries, Isabelle.

My feet shh-shh against the spring leaves; briars snag on my pants, then release. I have two miles to go to the main strip—I know where a back alley dead-ends at the forest that surrounds the town. A block or two, and I should have a vehicle; I'm adept at hot-wiring a car. Thirty seconds, and I'm on my way out of this town.

And once I get out of town, I'm all set. Ronnie booked me a spa appointment; he checked in himself last night so it'd look like I was there. Just in case.

He's a good man, which is probably why I'm not attracted to him. I have a soft spot for bad boys, and my preppy boy experiment with Jeff only solidified this instinct—from now on, a polo shirt will be enough to make me puke. But I am thankful that Ronnie leans tight-laced and proper. It made him help me, for one, but it also skewed his view of the world—and of me. He saw a kid-napper in Jeff, but he didn't see what I was. Because while I was down for a fling with a handsome silver fox I met at the amusement park, that certainly wasn't why I went home with him. I had plans for him before he locked me in that basement.

I still might be able to use the informa-tion I was able to find that first night. If not, I have another contingency plan. It does no good to be unprepared.

My breath burns in my lungs; my ribs ache. I hurry faster, slipping on dead leaves and the slime mold that proliferates beneath the rotting vegetation.

Snap!

I freeze—the sound is not me, nor is it squirrels. The crackling of branches.

Is Jeff after me? *Ronnie screwed up. I fucking knew he'd screw up.*

The rustling crackle comes again. Big— so big. Probably a deer. If it's a bear, it'll have to eat me before I'll go back to that house. Same if it's Jeff.

I steel myself and creep forward past low-rising brambles encased in a glittering thicket of thorns. In the distance, I can see a hazy lightening at the horizon, the sodium glare of streetlights along the strip. Half a mile away. Probably less.

I run toward the light—toward freedom. But the sound at my back follows.

Snap! Snap! Crunch!

So close now. I chance a look at my back,

but I see only the dark void of the trees, and though I do sense movement, I cannot make out any distinct shapes hidden in the velvet night.

Less than a quarter mile. I can see the brick retaining wall that separates the woods from the city proper, the edge where it drops off into cobblestones. I run harder, my back slick with sweat, my ribs vibrating with panic. The edge of the retaining wall approaches. I can't just run over the side; I'll have to jump.

I feel the dirt give way to cement beneath my sneakers. I leap out into the alley, my feet landing hard against the street. I tumble to my knees; skin rips, my knees tattooed by the cobbles, but it doesn't hurt, not with the way my heart is throbbing in my ears. I shove myself to my feet, still feeling as if the thing at my back is in pursuit, but when I whirl around, I see nothing in the shadow-blackened trees.

I made it. I made it.

But of course I did. I'm Isabelle fucking Cain. I'm a goddamn survivor.

The breeze hisses soft and sweet against the brick and brushes hard at my feverish flesh. No more noises come from the trees, but there is another sound now, too, scraping like claws on stone. I turn back to the alley—to freedom.

At first, I only see the blackness of the cobbles, the world hidden from streetlights, which is exactly why I chose it. Quiet here—isolated, as none of these businesses are open after five o'clock. But I am not alone. Amorphous shapes move through the inky haze—people? Yes, people, I realize as my eyes adjust. Delivery men, based on the boxes near their feet.

I squint, trying to force the scene to solidify. Four large men huddle in a knot against the right building, two of them crouching near the boxes. And now that my heart isn't thundering so violently, I can hear their agitated voices and the hissed scraping sound of the containers as they move them toward the vehicle—a truck, four now-dead running lights glinting in the moonlight that filters dimly between buildings.

I was not expecting to see anyone here, but unless I want to backtrack through the woods to the opposite end of town, I'll have to walk straight past them. And to walk all the way around will set me back thirty minutes that I do not have.

I frown. I don't think they can identify me here in the dark, and I don't think they'll connect me to Jeff—I'm two miles from his home, and my presence here is circumstantial at best. These men are very unlikely to hear about Jeff's death at all if they don't live in Haling Cove. And even if they do, I'll be long gone before they can tell anyone.

I square my shoulders and head in their direction, but between the wind and the rumble of their truck's idling engine, and their own raised voices, I don't think they can hear the dull patter of my rubber-soled footwear. None of them are facing me—their heads are all turned away, two of them crouched near the boxes at the wall.

I pick up my pace. Thirty feet away.

My mouth is packed in cotton. Twenty feet.

I freeze. This close, I can see what they're loading.

I had thought they were moving boxes, but it's not boxes, the shapes too misshapen —bags. And what I thought was a running board isn't the back lights of a waiting truck. Motorcycles, four of them, lined up in a row.

The other images come in slowly pulsing flashes. The back door beside them is a dull, hazy silver. Something glitters on the ground like a string of diamonds. Actually... maybe it is diamonds. A necklace?

The jewelry store. They're robbing the jewelry store. They don't acknowledge my presence.

But then... one does.

The man nearest me stands slowly. They're all in black, head to toe, which is why I thought I was looking at the back of his head, but now I can see the glitter of two eyes beneath his mask. A ski mask? No, a helmet, visor up. He steps toward me, away from the fray, and as he moves from the knot of men, I can see beyond him. I can see what lays at their feet.

The man on the ground isn't nearly as large as the robbers, and not nearly as alive. His eyes were wide to the moon, his gaze dull—unseeing. The puddle beneath his head is still spreading, inky black, but I can smell it now, the metallic reek of blood. And the bikers—the murderers—are all staring. Straight at me.

The biggest of them points, his body silhouetted by the light from the main drag—impossibly far away. "Take her."

GET *TAKEN* ON RBFIELDS.COM!

**They kidnapped her
to keep her safe.
Now they want to
make her theirs.**

BORN OF DARKNESS

BECKONED
Born of Darkness, Book #1

"Steamy reverse harem for fans of Laurell K. Hamilton."

CHAPTER 1
Dawn

My mother used to tell me I was born to the dark; that's mostly bullshit.

But I am drawn to it. It's weird the way it wakes me some nights, shadows slithering through my veins like oil, seeping out from the hidden places inside me where no one else can see. Dawn is a weird name for a woman like that, a woman so immersed in darkness, but I think my mom was trying to fight against what she already knew — that I wasn't like her.

I'm not like most people.

I walk, the thumping of my black boots on the splintered wood of the boardwalk making a sound like that of an angry bull-frog. The thin line of lights they've strung above the boardwalk sways, and the shadows undulate, a million ghosts trying to find footing before the breeze whips the light away, making the ghostly shadows vanish into the water below. I guess I've always had a vivid imagination. Maybe I should have been an author, a playwright, a musician, some particularly creative brand of person who spends their days on fanciful pursuits, who loves life and flowers and puppies — I mean, not that I don't love puppies. What kind of monster wouldn't love those fuzzy bastards? I'm only human, after all. But the monsters ...

I know them when I see them.

I've been a nurse for ten years, and I'll never get used to the injuries or the heartache that often comes with them. And no matter how fast I stitch, there's always one more asshole ready to destroy the people I want to help, whether it's a woman beaten senseless by her lover or a kid abused by his parents — a man run into a tree by some dickhead with road rage. I'm not perfect by any means; I'm one pill away from a quick slide to hell. I used to think the drugs would take the edge off, but it never lasts.

But this high will last, at least for a little while. I'm pretty sure this isn't what my mother wanted for me, raising me alone — she tried so hard to keep me away from monsters.

And here I am, wandering toward them.

This stretch of bridge has been the hunting ground for someone more vicious than the domestic abusers who show up at the hospital to kiss their wives after they've roughed them up. A serial killer, they think, strangling women and tossing them from the bridge — three have washed up on shore, the same fine band of bruising around their throats, their chests and bellies torn open, organs missing, intestines shredded. The guy I'm after is probably just responsible for the strangulation, though; it's most likely that an animal lurking beneath the bridge is responsible for the rest, ripping up the scraps the murderer tosses down — a symbiotic relationship between killer and wildlife. I can still hear the newscaster's voice in my head: *Police say the Breakwater Bridge is hazardous and have imposed a curfew — no foot traffic is allowed on the bridge after seven p.m.*

But not everyone can avoid the bridge, which means there will be more victims unless I stop him. The police force in this tiny

Maine town can't patrol the boardwalk — it would take all night to walk up and down, and there are only two deputies on duty, and at least one of them needs to be stationed outside the town's only bar. Clarence Church will be beating the shit out of someone come eleven o'clock, nine on the weekend. And there's not another good way home if you work on the peninsula. On a busy weekend night, it takes forty-five minutes by car to take the clogged two-lane street around the water — the peninsula, what the kids call "the penis," juts out far enough that a bridge over the rocky shoreline is the fastest way back to civilization, and the long stretch of beach under the bridge is made of gray stones that are treacherous on a good day but vicious in the dark. Anyone trying to take a shortcut beneath the bridge would likely kill themselves in the surf.

But it's Tuesday now; no one's working tonight. The Ferris wheel is dark on the pier, just a skeleton outline that I wouldn't have been able to see if not for the silvery moon.

This is when he'll hunt, I can feel it in my bones, but it's also logical — he hasn't been caught yet, which means there's no way he's hunting when it's busy.

The ocean roars, salty and cold — I can almost hear ice in the autumn tide. I can hear the rocks too, the way the waves throw themselves onto their sharp surfaces, uncaring, ready to be cleaved apart for just one moment of freedom, one taste of raw air. Like me, I guess. Catching a homicidal maniac ... it's exhilarating. I've caught three killers so far, but any one of them might be the one that kills me. Any one of them might see me. I'm not sure why I haven't been snatched up yet, but my mom always said I was sneaky, and that's probably true based on the current evidence.

But there's nowhere to hide on this long stretch of bridge, not so much as a garbage can to obscure my presence, and only the noise of the surf to cover my footsteps. Quiet — good. Ever since my mother died, I've been partial to silence. Something about hearing her being torn apart — serial killers, amiright? Probably not a shocker that I've made it my life's mission to put these assholes out of commission. I wouldn't wish the things I've seen on my worst enemy, except maybe Marcy Miller, who showed my panties to our whole third-grade class. That hoe has it coming.

I stop in the middle of the bridge and listen to the song of the ocean, the accompanying whistle of the rushing wind pushed around by the tides. Seconds pass. Minutes. Bitter wind bites at my nose. The Ferris wheel vanishes when the clouds obscure the moon, then glints back into being. A dove coos at me from the railing, brilliant red eyes glaring — it's watching me. The skin between my shoulders prickles. The bird flutters off into the night as if it feels my tension and wants to escape it.

And then I hear him — footsteps.

Thud, thud, thud.

It sounds like a heartbeat, and my heart responds in kind, matching every throbbing movement of his shoes — more a sixth sense born of having to watch your back. Between the hospital and my mother, I know bad actors abound; even my own father sounds like a real piece of work. I sometimes wonder if my dad raped my mom, if that's my real legacy, but I never asked her. And I sure as hell can't ask her now.

And then ... nothing. My heart pauses. Silence sighs through my veins, thick and heavy. And then the throbbing is back. The tap of the man's shoes draws closer — is it him? The Boardwalk Butcher? I don't know for sure, not yet, but I raise my fingertips to my hip where I keep my mother's knife. The leather is chill and damp and has never felt more like skin. The blade's edge and the symbols carved along the sides are hot, though — they're always hot because, by the time I reach for it, my adrenaline is already pumping like a firehose through my veins.

The dull tapping of leather on wood comes again, louder, wetter — *thwack, thwack, thwack*. I click the snap and unsheathe the blade. I've always been more comfortable with a knife than with a gun. I'm more agile than most of the assholes I catch, and martial arts has forged me into a better fighter than, say, a dickhead who needs a wire to strangle a woman on a bridge.

I push myself off the railing and turn away from the sound of his feet — still too far to be dangerous. If he starts running, I'll run too. I'm fast as hell, and I can have the police on either end of this bridge by the time I get to the parking lot that marks the end of the boardwalk.

But I only take a few steps before my heart leaps into my throat. The man behind me is not the only one on the bridge. In the distance, another man is approaching. There's no reason for anyone to be out here, not now, and despite his broad-shouldered frame, the boots on his feet, I did not hear his footsteps approaching over the rickety surface of the bridge. A dark hoodie hides most of his face, but I can see the chiseled line of his jaw; faded jeans cling loosely to his hips. He raises his head, and his gaze meets mine, eyes violet in the silvery moonlight.

The footsteps behind me accelerate.

The man in front of me smiles.

Two of them. There are two of them out here on a night no one should be on the bridge. Are there two killers, a tag team of maniacs? The police hadn't considered this, and neither had I. *Shit.* This isn't how it's supposed to go.

I slip the knife free of its holster and clutch it to my abdomen, ready to raise it if I have to — the stranger in front of me is twenty feet and closing, and from behind me, the spread thrum of footsteps carries on, *thud-thwack-thud.* I pick up my pace, muscles like steel, eyes narrowed, but when I blink ...

Huh. I squint, scanning the boardwalk, but I see only the moon-washed boards, the rail on either side, the black horizon of the parking lot in the distance. The man in front of me is gone. But there's nowhere for a man to go unless he flung himself over the railing. I almost laugh — of course my brain would invent a handsome stranger on a long lonesome bridge. Not only is this exactly the kind of situation that screams "damsel in distress," but I haven't had sex in months.

I listen to the footsteps behind me — closer. Closer. Who needs sex when you can bag a killer?

Thudthwackthwack, faster now, still far enough back that I'm not in danger yet, but time is of the essence. I run. The parking lot seems so far away, but I've got the stamina. I clutch the knife in one hand and thumb my cell phone on with the other. *9-1* —

The pain comes out of nowhere, a blinding flash of agony like white-hot poker stabbing into my brain. I don't remember falling, but I'm on my knees, the wood splintering against my shins, my head an aching, throbbing ball of light. No, there's no way, he was so far back — how did he get here so fast?

It's impossible, but undeniable — I'm on the ground, my head aching where he smashed something into my skull.

And he's above me.

I can smell him, an old muskiness like mildew mingling with the metallic tang of fear. Dizziness tugs at me, trying to pull me to the earth — my ears are ringing. And the phone ... I see it, the screen blinking at the sky ten feet up the boardwalk. I imagine how I might look dashed against the rocks, my dark hair hiding the blood. That thin line of purple around my neck. My heart ripped clean out of my chest.

I squint, trying to focus my eyes, but they refuse; all I can do is listen. His breath is like the growl of a monster, but I can't tell exactly where he is. It's as if his breath is coming from everywhere and nowhere at once, whisking around me in a tornado of hatred. It should be nothing more than a hissed whispering barely noticeable above the roar of the surf, but I swear it's like he's screaming at me — I hear the blood in his veins, too, the whooshing of each individual air sac in his lungs. I hear how desperately he wants to kill me. It's weird how it doesn't scare me — death. I don't hate my life, I don't, but it's just never felt like ... well, enough.

Sorry, Mom, I know you wanted more

than this for me. I'll be apologizing to her in person soon enough. Well, not "person," I guess. In ... ghost? But I don't believe in ghosts.

I do believe in evil. My spine goes rigid.

I'm not dying on this fucking bridge.

I blink, the fuzzy haze dissipating from the corners of my vision, and launch myself forward, skittering up the boardwalk, the knife still clenched tightly against my ribs — if I can get to the phone, maybe I can alert the police. I'm not sure what other choice I have; if I climb over the rail, I'll die on the rocks below just as surely as I'll die here, but at least I won't give that fuckstick the satisfaction of killing me.

Splinters stab into my kneecaps. The phone is a weight in my hand. His breath ... Is he gone? I can't see, the world beyond the phone looks dark with shadows, and even if that's my eyes ... I don't hear him. Can't hear anything but the wind and the pulse of panic in my brain. My fingers shake as I tap the buttons, *9-1-1, sen* —

The phone skitters away as he grabs my

arm just below the shoulder, wrenching it from the socket. I grind my teeth to avoid screaming — *because fuck him, that's why* — and use his stability to haul myself against his arm as I twist, pulling my fist from the earth and slamming the butt of the knife into his balls. Usually, a shot to the taint puts a man on his knees, but he doesn't seem to feel it; his grip doesn't waver. His nails are steel spikes against my bicep, sharp — too sharp — tearing my skin.

But I won't scream. I won't give him that.

Dizzy — so dizzy.

I go limp for one heartbeat, long enough for him to shift right. He's at my back, one hand on my arm, his shoes squared behind my hips. I tighten my fingers on the blade. *One.* I breathe — deeply, purposefully. *Two.* I tense my muscles, preparing.

Now.

I whip the knife back into his thigh, feel the blade ram into his flesh. I know I hurt him this time; his hand slips from my injured shoulder. I jerk away, scrambling up the boardwalk. I can't see the end anymore. Too far — much too far.

He roars like an animal, a low rumble deep in his chest, but he does not stop moving. He lunges for me, staggering, dragging his injured leg. The knife falls from his flesh and clatters to the wood. I throw an elbow, whipping my body his way, and lash out with my opposite fist, connecting with his hip, but again, it does not phase him — it's like hitting stone. And I can't fucking see him; his face is dark beneath his hood. But I can hear him. His breath is ragged as if he has marbles in his lungs — as if he's dying — but I know that's too much to ask for. Every martial arts lesson, every day of training, and it was all for nothing. The world wavers, a kaleidoscope pattern of the boardwalk planks, and the far-off Ferris wheel, the dim yellow glint of a lighthouse well past its prime.

I feel the metal around my throat.

The world solidifies. I look at the sky, the blanket of stars. The killer behind me pulls the wire tighter. Heat pours into my face as the blood freezes in my veins. Darkness encroaches on the edges of my vision. I flail at him, but every time I move, the band around my throat grows tighter. The world is shrouded in darkness — I can't even see my own knees.

And suddenly, the pressure is gone, the roar of the surf is gone, and all I can hear is a horrific screaming like that of a thousand demons — or what I imagine they might sound like. Am I dying? Is this what it feels like? But no, the pain is all still there, the horrid ache in the back of my skull, the stinging pain from my tattered arm, the burning in my lungs, but the air ... It's rushing into my chest, and I can see my hands, the wood beneath, the bloody nub where one of my fingernails used to be.

The screaming stops. The surf roars. And while there is no screaming, there is another sound, a wet tearing sound, and that noise ... I know that noise. I can see my mother on the floor; I can hear the monster above her. But that was just a dream.

This is real.

I push myself onto my knees and finally turn my head. A sharp pain sears through my throat — dizziness tugs at me once more. But through the film of my wavering vision, I can make out the shape of a man ... No. Two men, one on the ground, the other crouched above him. A heavyset man with tousled blonde hair lays on the boardwalk, his black hood puddled on the planks, a wire wrapped around his fingers. The wire that should have killed me. So familiar, that man — where have I seen him before? Is it my imagination? I shudder when I meet his eyes, but he's not staring at me — he's looking through me. Dead, he's dead, that fucker.

But the man above him ...

The man on the boardwalk — he's real, he's real, too — is hunched over the killer, the thick ropey muscles of his shoulders wrestling beneath the cloth of his sweatshirt, his face hidden behind the bulk of his shoulders. He leans lower, and the killer's arm jerks, too, and ... What is he doing? Giving him CPR? *Don't help him, that asshole deserves to die!* But if they were partners ...

I swallow hard and ease backward, reaching for the phone, snatching up the knife, ready, ready, but I'm not as steady as I need to be. I grit my teeth.

The crouched man freezes abruptly as if he senses me watching and draws himself to standing, giving me a better view of the man on the boardwalk. The killer's black sweatshirt doesn't show blood, but I can see it on the wood beneath, staining the planks in brilliant crimson. The crater of his abdomen gapes, a bloody hole edged in shattered ribs and yellow fat and a large piece of meat that might be his liver.

Goddammit. I came here for a serial killer and ended up with a werewolf. Awesome.

But there's no fur — he should have fur. Instead, he's pale, chiseled, every feature honed in marble. Except for those eyes. Those violet eyes. A trick of the light?

I can't breathe. His feet make no sound as he draws nearer, but there's something about him ... he feels older than the walking path beneath us, the way the ocean feels old, the way the dirt and stone feel heavy with unknowable wisdom — as if he's seen more than any mortal ever could.

The man looks down at me and blinks. Violet eyes, not just from the light — I'm sure. The glow is coming from inside them, reflected like a lion. Like a hunter. His teeth are long, pointed — wickedly sharp.

His face is covered in blood.

GET *BECKONED* ON RBFIELDS.COM!

"Steamy. If you like Anita Blake, you'll love this series!"

ROOM ON TOP

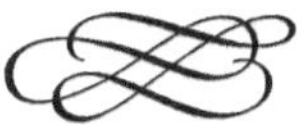

Do you love short stories? There are plenty to choose from.

Jess is a stalwart legal professional, a rising star at a multi-million dollar firm. The icing on the cake is that her bosses are easy on the eyes—alphas in every sense of that phrase. Not that she'd ever do anything about that, of course... no matter how much she wants to.

But when a rude client pushes her over the

edge, Jess finds herself in uncharted territory—she's lost the firm their biggest client. And now she has to explain it to the partners.

But she never anticipated tonight's business meeting would go this way.

What her bosses want, her bosses get.

And she's more than happy to work late.

GET "ROOM ON TOP" ON RBFIELDS.COM!

ABOUT THE AUTHOR

R. B. Fields is a clinical therapist turned romance author and has never shied away from the multitude of ways couples can enhance their love lives. She is currently using this knowledge to write about the rich tapestry of fantasies inherent to the human experience. Learn more on https://rbfield s.com!